Edwin Arnold

A Simple Transliteral Grammar of the Turkish Language

Edwin Arnold

A Simple Transliteral Grammar of the Turkish Language

ISBN/EAN: 9783337294786

Printed in Europe, USA, Canada, Australia, Japan

Cover: Foto ©Andreas Hilbeck / pixelio.de

More available books at **www.hansebooks.com**

A SIMPLE

TRANSLITERAL GRAMMAR

OF THE

TURKISH LANGUAGE.

Compiled from Various Sources.

WITH DIALOGUES AND VOCABULARY.

BY

EDWIN ARNOLD, M.A., C.S.I., F.R.G.S.

LONDON:

TRÜBNER & CO., LUDGATE HILL.

1877.

PREFACE.

THIS little book is merely a compilation formed by the author in his own study of Turkish, and offered to other beginners as an aid towards acquaintance with that language, in the present singular dearth of Turkish grammars and instruction books. The Eastern Problem has re-arisen in an absorbing manner to give new interest to a tongue spoken over so vast and important an Empire; while—apart from the advantage to the politician, the journalist, the educated Englishman, and the traveller of some knowledge of the Ottoman language—it is, for its own sake, well worth a scholar's passing attention, being scientific in structure and in composition clear, concise, and expressive. These rules, forms, dialogues, and vocabularies are condensed from many sources, with intent to convey that degree of knowledge upon which a limited but useful power of conversation can be built. The attempt has been made to dispense with the Oriental character altogether, since it is something at least to learn the grammatical architecture of a spoken language, and the ear then becomes a tutor to the eye. The difficulty of representing the Turkish letters could not have been quite overcome without fuller details; but further study must supply precision, and in the present unassuming sketch the author aims at no credit except that of simplicity, and to render a small service in the great matter of " Justice to Islam."

London, *February* 1877.

CONTENTS.

PART I.

CONTENTS.

PART II.

PART III.

OUTLINES

OF

TURKISH GRAMMAR.

———

PART I.

The Alphabet and its Pronunciation.

Turkish Letters.	English Sound.	Turkish Letters.	English Sound.	Turkish Letters.	English Sound.
ا	A	ز	Z	ق	K
ب	B	ژ	J	ك	K
پ	P	س	S	ك	nasal n *
ت	T	ش	Sh	ك	Gu
ث	S	ص	S	ل	L
ج	Dj	ض	Z	م	M
چ	Tch	ط	T	ن	N
ح	H	ظ	Z	و	V, O, U
خ	Kh	ع	soft breathing	ه	H
د	D	غ	guttural g and h	ى	I, Y, a
ذ	Z	ف	F	ال	La
ر	R				

A

1. The Turkish alphabet contains twenty-eight Arabic characters, four Persian, and one only of native origin—the "deaf *n*"—(marked *): in all thirty-three; Lam-Alif, the last, being a compound. The letters are here shown in their simple form—they alter their shape in the middle and at the end of words: their pronunciation is generally that here given opposite each letter. Turkish is read from right to left. The vowels, supplied by marks above and below the letters, are commonly omitted in writing. As this sketch of the language aims to teach by transcription, no time need be lost over these points. Turkish, though simple, is expressive and scientific in construction; and, on many accounts, a language worth studying for its own sake.

NOUNS.

2. Turkish has no article, but the indefinite *bir*, a, an, one, is sometimes used.

Turkish nouns have no gender. Distinctions of sex, when not conveyed in the word itself, are marked by *oghlan* for male and *kiz* for female in human relations; by *erkek*, male, and *dishi*, female, for animals.

Turkish nouns have two numbers—singular and plural. Their cases are formed by terminal variations. The plural is made by adding *lar* or *ler* to the singular—the first after a hard consonant, the second after a soft one.

Turkish nouns are of two kinds—those ending in a consonant, as *vezir*, *calpak*, and those in a vowel-sound, as *baba*, father ; *capoo*, gate ; *dereh*, village.

DECLENSION OF CONSONANTAL NOUNS.

Singular.

Nom.	*vezir*,	the minister.
Gen.	*vezirun*,	of the minister.
Dat.	*vezireh*,	to the minister.
Acc.	*veziry*,	the minister.
Voc.	*ya vezir*,	O minister.
Abl.	*vezirdan*,	from the minister.

Plural.

Nom.	*vezirler*,	the ministers.
Gen.	*vezirlerun*,	of the ministers.
Dat.	*vezirlereh*,	to the ministers.
Acc.	*vezirlery*,	the ministers.
Voc.	*ya vezirler*,	O ministers.
Abl.	*vezirlerden*,	from the ministers.

DECLENSION OF VOWEL-NOUNS.

Singular.

Nom.	baba,	the father.
Gen.	babanun,	of the father.
Dat.	babayah,	to the father.
Acc.	babayi,	the father.
Voc.	ya baba,	O father.
Abl.	babadan,	from the father.

Plural.

Nom.	babalar,	the fathers.
Gen.	babalarun,	of the fathers.
Dat.	babalarah,	to the fathers.
Acc.	babalary,	the fathers.
Voc.	ya babalar,	O fathers.
Abl.	babalardan,	from the fathers.

Thus vowel-nouns add *nun* (*nin*), *yah*, *yi*, and *dan* to the nominative singular for genitive, dative, accusative, and ablative, while consonant-nouns add for the three first cases *un* (*in*), *ah* or *eh*, and *i* or *y*.

There are a few exceptions, but they need not occupy any space in this slight sketch. The plurals are necessarily regular, being like nouns ending in *r*.

ADJECTIVES.

Turkish adjectives have no inflections, either for gender or number, except when used as substantives. They stand before their nouns, and are unchanged, in this way :

Singular.

Nom.	*guzel el*	the pretty hand.
Gen.	*guzel elun*	of the pretty hand.
Dat.	*guzel elah*	to the pretty hand.
Acc.	*guzel ely*	the pretty hand.
Voc.	*ya guzel el*	O pretty hand.
Abl.	*guzel eldan*	from the pretty hand.

Plural.

Nom.	*guzel eller*	the pretty hands.
Gen.	*guzel ellerun*	of the pretty hands.
Dat.	*guzel ellerah*	to the pretty hands.
Acc.	*guzel ellery*	the pretty hands.
Voc.	*ya guzel eller*	O pretty hands.
Abl.	*guzel ellerdan*	from the pretty hands.

Turkish adjectives form their degrees as follows :—

The comparative is made by adding *djeh* or *tcheh* to the positive, as

ḡuzel, handsome ; *guzeldjeh*, handsomer.

(*eyi*) *eiu*, good ; *eiutcheh*, better.

Or by putting *daha*, more, before the adjective, as

buyuk, large ; *daha buyuk*, larger.

zenguin, rich ; *daha zenguin*, richer.

Or by the ablative, followed by the adjective, as

kalemdan guzel, finer than a pen.

kalpakdan buyuk, larger than a hood.

sen benden eyi sen, thou art better than I.

The superlative is made by putting the noun in the genitive or ablative, and adding *y* to the adjective if it end in a consonant, and *sy* if it end in a vowel. Thus

babanun eyusy, best of fathers.

kieupeyun fenasy, the worst dog.

avretlerun guzely, handsomest of women.

Superlatives are also expressed by placing before the adjective the particles *en, pek, ziadeh, ghairet*, which thus all mean " exceedingly." These may even be coupled, as

pek ziadeh, the most.

The Turks also obtain the idea of superlativeness by doubling the adjective or adverb as cumulative epithets. Thus

pek pek, very much.

sek sek, very often.

tchok tchok eyu adam, a very, very good man.

Besides their primitive nouns the Turks commonly form nouns from verbs and adjectives. Thus "nouns agent" are made by adding *djy* or *idjy* to the second sing. imperative of the verb. As

> *sevidjy*, a lover, from *sev*, love thou.
>
> *koortardjy*, a saviour, from *koortar*, save thou.

The "nouns acted" are made either by dropping the last letters of the infinitive, as

> *eulm*, death, from *eulmek*, to die.

Or by changing the *mak* or *mek* of the infinitive into *sh* or *ish*, as

> *almak*, to receive; *alish*, receipt.
>
> *gurmek*, to see; *gursh*, sight.

Or by *eh* or *ah* substituted for the *k* of the infinitive, as

> *bilmeh*, knowledge, from *bilmek*, to know.
>
> *anmah*, memory, from *anmak*, to remember.

Or by adding *lik* to the infinitive, as

> *bilmek*, to know; *bilmeklik*, knowledge.
>
> *yemek*, to eat; *yemeklik*, food.

Adjectives are made from nouns—and nouns also—by adding *lu* or *ly* to the nominative. Thus *mal*, wealth ; *mallu*, wealthy.

gumush, silver ; *gumushly*, silvered.

Venedik, Venice ; *Venedikly*, a Venetian.

tooz, salt ; *toozly*, salt-savoured.

at, horse ; *atlu*, a horseman.

The particle *djy* denotes trade or action. Thus

kaik, boat ; *kaikdjy*, boatman.

yol, road ; *yoldjy*, traveller.

etmek, bread ; *etmekdjy*, baker.

The particle *lik* is added to nouns or adjectives to form new substantives. Thus

guzel, beautiful ; *guzelik*, beauty.

pasha, governor ; *pashalik*, the government.

dost, friend ; *dostlik*, friendship.

yeni, new; *yenilik*, novelty.

As also for localities. Thus

donooz, pig ; *donoozlik*, pig-stye.

azum, grape ; *azmlik*, vineyard.

Diminutives are obtained by adding *djek* or *djuk* to nouns, and *djeh*, *djah*, or *tcheh* to adjectives. Thus

adam, a man ; *adamdjek*, a dwarf.

kutchuk, small ; *kutchuktcheh*, very small.

And from these are made terms of endearment by adding *ez*, as

babadjek, little father ; *babadjaghez*, dearest father.
atdjek, a pony ; *atdjeghez*, pretty little nag.

Finally, by adding *siz*, without, to nouns the idea of deprivation is expressed, as

dost, a friend ; *dostsiz*, friendless.

djan, life ; *djansiz*, lifeless.

[Many postpositions are thus used.]

NUMBERS.

The cardinal numbers are—

1. *bir*	11. *on bir*	30. *otooz*
2. *iki*	12. *on iki*	40. *kirk*
3. *iitch*	13. *on utch*	50. *elli*
4. *deurt*	14. *on deurt*	60. *altmish*
5. *besh*	15. *on besh*	70. *yetmish*
6. *alti*	16. *on alti*	80. *sekzen*
7. *yedi*	17. *on yedi*	90. *doksan*
8. *sekiz*	18. *on sekiz*	100. *yuz*
9. *dokooz*	19. *on dokooz*	1000. *bin*
10. *on*	20. *iyirmi*	100,000. *yuz bin*

N.B.—In ciphering, the Turks write and read figures, as with us, from left to right.

The ordinal numbers are formed by adding *indjy* to the cardinal. Thus

birindjy,	first.	*oonoonindjy,*	tenth.
ikindjy,	second.	*iyirmindjy,*	twentieth.
utchindjy,	third.	*binindjy,*	thousandth.
deurtindjy,	fourth.		

These are declinable, as

utchindjylerun iki, two of the thirds.

Fractional parts are *yarem*, a half (or *boot-chook*), and *tcherek*, a quarter, as

yarem sa'at, half an hour.

tcherek yol, a fourth of the way.

iki bootchook ghroush, two piastres and a half.

The particle *er* or *sher* repeats a number, as

birer, one by one.

ikisher, two by two.

Keri multiplies, as

iki keri, twice.

besh keri, five times.

For numbers of persons, animals, and things the Turks use the different words respectively *kishi*, *bash*, and *tana*. Thus

yuz bin kishiler, 100,000 men.

iki yuz bashler, 200 head (of cattle).

elli bin tana, 50,000 pieces (of cloth).

Kat or *keder* answers to " fold," as

utch keder, threefold.

tchok kat, manifold.

———

PRONOUNS

Are —(1) personal, (2) possessive, (3) demonstrative, (4) relative, (5) interrogative, (6) indefinite.

N.B.—The vocative case is omitted below as it is simply the nominative with *ya* prefixed.

1. Personal Pronouns are

FIRST PERSON.

Singular.		*Plural.*	
Nom.	*ben*, I.	*biz*, we.	
Gen.	*benim*, of me.	*bizim*, of us.	
Dat.	*bana*, to me.	*bizeh*, to us.	
Acc.	*beni*, me.	*bizi*, us.	
Abl.	*benden*, from me.	*bizden*, from us.	

SECOND PERSON.

Singular.			*Plural.*	
Nom.	*sen*,	thou.	*siz*,	you.
Gen.	*senun*,	of thee.	*sizun*,	of you.
Dat.	*sana*,	to thee.	*sizeh*,	to you.
Acc.	*seni*,	thee.	*sizi*,	you.
Abl.	*senden*,	from thee.	*sizden*,	from you.

THIRD PERSON.
Singular.

Nom. o', o,   he, she, it.
Gen. onoon, anoon,   of him, her, &c.
Dat. ana,   to him, &c.
Acc. ani, onoo,   him, &c.
Abl. anden, ondan,   from him, &c.

Plural.

Nom. anlar, onlar,   them.
Gen. anlarun, onlarun,   of them.
Dat. anlareh, onlareh,   to them.
Acc. anlari, onlari,   them.
Abl. anlarden, onlardan,   from them.

2. THE POSSESSIVE PRONOUNS are the genitives of the personal pronouns. Thus

> *benim,* my ; *bizim,* our.
> *senun* or *senin,* thy ; *sizun,* your.
> *onoon,* his ; *onlarun,* their.

They are indeclinable.

But the Turks cut these short, and join the abbreviated sign to a noun in order to denote possession, using for

mine—*m, im, um.*   ours—*miz, imiz.*
thine—*n, in, un.*   yours—*niz, iniz.*
his, her, its—*i, y, u.*   theirs—*i, y, u.*

Examples :—

baba, father, makes *babam*, my father.

kitab, book,   ,,   *kitabim*, my book.

ev, house,   ,,   *evun*, thy house.

kalam, pen,   ,,   *kalamimiz*, our pen.

huzret, worship, ,, *huzretiniz*, your worship.

cooler, slave,   ,,   *coolery*, their slaves.

These compounds may be declined like an ordinary substantive. Thus

carndashimizeh, to our brother.

dostundan, from thy friend.

The absolute possessives, mine, thine, &c., are represented by the genitive followed by *ki*, as

benimki, mine ; *seninki*, thine.

bizimki, ours ; *anlarunki*, theirs.

3. DEMONSTRATIVE PRONOUNS are

shoo, this, that.   *o*,   that.

boo, this.   *ol*,   that.

ishboo, this.   *kendi*, himself.

Thus,

Singular.

Nom.	*boo, shoo, ishboo,*	this, that.
Gen.	*boonoon,*	of this.
Dat.	*boonah,*	to this.
Acc.	*booni,*	this.
Abl.	*boondan,*	from this.

Plural.

Nom. *boonlar,*   these.
Gen. *boonlarun,*   of them.
Dat. *boonlarah,*   to them,
Acc. *boonlari,*   these.
Abl. *boonlardan,*   from these.

(O and *ol* have already been declined as personal pronouns.)

Kendi has slight variations.

Singular.

Nom. *kendi,*   himself.
Gen. *kendunin,*   of himself.
Dat. *kenduyeh, kendineh,*   to himself.
Acc. *kenduyi, kendiny,*   himself.
Abl. *kendinden, kendooden,* from himself.

Plural.

Nom. *kendiler,*   themselves.
Gen. *kendulerun,*   of themselves.
Dat. *kendulereh,*   to themselves.
Acc. *kenduleri,*   themselves.
Abl. *kendulerden,*   from themselves.

4. THE RELATIVE PRONOUN *kih,* who, which, what, is not declinable, but it is joined to personal pronouns sometimes for inflection, as

kih anun, of whom ; *kih ondan,* from whom.

5. THE INTERROGATIVE PRONOUNS are *kim*, who? *neh*, what? *Kim* is declined—

Singular.

Nom.	*kim,*	who, which.
Gen.	*kimun,*	of whom, which.
Dat.	*kimeh,*	to whom, which.
Acc.	*kimi,*	whom, which.
Abl.	*kimden,*	from whom, which.

Plural.

Nom.	*kimler,*	who, which.
Gen.	*kimlerun,*	of whom, which.
Dat.	*kimlereh,*	to whom, which.
Acc.	*kimleri,*	. whom, which.
Abl.	*kimlerdan,*	from whom, which.

Neh, what? is thus declined—

Singular.

Nom.	*neh,*	what.
Gen.	*nehnun,*	of what.
Dat.	*nehyeh,*	to what.
Acc.	*nehy,*	what.
Abl.	*nehden,*	from what.

Plural.

Nom.	*nehler,*	what, which.
Gen.	*nehlerun,*	of what, which.

Dat.	*nehlereh,*	to what, which.
Acc.	*nehleri.*	what, which.
Abl.	*nehlerdan,*	from what, which.

Neh preceding an adjective signifies " how "—

neh guzel, how handsome.

neh mootlu, how happy.

Neh also takes the possessive signs, as—

nehmiz var, what have we got ?

Kanghy, " which " (indeclinable), should also be mentioned—

kanghy at, which horse ?

kanghi miz, which of us ?

6. INDEFINITE PRONOUNS are

bir kimseh,
bir kishi, } some one.

kajri, whatever.

hehr,   all.   *beuteun,* all.

hehr biri,
hehr kess. } ; each, all.
hepissi,

hitch bir kimseh,   no one.

hitch bir shey,   nothing.

filan,   such an one.

ol bir,   the other.

hehr kim, ⎫
hehr kanghy, ⎬   whoever.

hehr neh,   whatever.

These pronouns are undeclined.

VERBS.

Turkish verbs would appear formidable if dis-
played in all their voices and varieties; but these
are best learnt after some familiarity with the
spoken language. Only the very simplest forms
and rules will be given here. Almost all the
tenses are made from the second person of the
imperative.

All regular verbs have the infinitive in *mak* if
the preceding syllable has *o* or *u*, or *mek* if it has
i or *e*, the first taking *a* in conjugating, the last
e; as

> *kosamak,* to fly, gives *kosarim,* I fly.
>
> *sevmek,* to love, gives *severim,* I love.

Besides the active and passive voices, Turkish
has many others; but those most necessary for
practical purposes are, next to the above, the negative, impotential, causal, reciprocal, and reflected.

To form the passive from the active, it is

necessary to place *il* after the root of the verb, which in Turkish is easily recognised ; as

sermek, to love ; *serilmek*, to be loved.

To form the negative, it is necessary to place *me* or *ma* after the root ; as

sermek, to love ; *sermemek*, not to love.
atmak, to throw ; *atmamak*, not to throw.

To form the impotential, it is necessary to place *eme* or *ama* after the root ; as

sermek, to love; *serememek*, not to be able to love.
bakamamak, to be incapable of seeing.

To form the causal, it is necessary to place *dir*, *tir*, or *t* after the root ; as

sermek, to love ; *serdirmek*, to cause to love.
okumak, to read ; *okutmak*, to make to read.

To form the reciprocal, it is necessary to place *ish* after the root ; as

sermek, to love ; *sevishmek*, to love one another.

To form the reflected, *un* or *in* is written after the root ; as

gurmek, to see ; *gurinmek*, to see oneself.

After this explanation, it will suffice to give the active voice of one regular verb.

FIRST CONJUGATION OF REGULAR VERBS
in **mek**.

INFINITIVE, *sermek*, to love.

INDICATIVE MOOD.

PRESENT TENSE.

Singular.		*Plural.*	
severim,	I love.	*severiz,*	we love.
seversen,	thou lovest.	*seversiz,*	ye love.
sever,	he loves.	*severler,*	they love.

IMPERFECT.

Singular.		*Plural.*	
severdim,	I did love.	*severduk,*	we did love.
severdin,	thou didst love.	*severdiniz,*	ye did love.
severdi,	he did love.	*severdiler,*	they did love.

PRETERITE TENSE.
Singular.

sevdim,	I have loved.
sevdin,	thou hast loved.
sevdi,	he has loved.

Plural.

sevduk,	we have loved.
sevdinez,	ye have loved.
sevdiler,	they have loved.

PLUPERFECT TENSE.

Singular.

sevmishidim,	I had loved.
sevmishidin,	thou hadst loved.
sevmishidi,	he had loved.

Plural.

sevmishiduk,	we had loved.
sevmishidinez,	ye had loved.
sevmishidler,	they had loved.

FUTURE TENSE.

Singular.

sevejeim,	I shall love.
sevejeksin,	thou shalt love.
sevejekder,	he shall love.

Plural.

sevejeiz,	we shall love.
sevejeksiz,	ye shall love.
sevejeklerder,	they shall love.

SUBJUNCTIVE MOOD.

PRESENT TENSE.

Singular.

eyer seversim,	if I love.
eyer seversen,	if thou lovest.
eyer seversè,	if he loves.

Plural.

eyer seversek,	if we love.
eyer seversiniz,	if ye love.
eyer seversèler,	if they love.

IMPERFECT TENSE.

Singular.

eyer sevsim,	if I loved.
eyer sevsen,	if thou lovedst.
eyer sevsè,	if he loves.

Plural.

eyer sevsek,	if we loved.
eyer sevsiniz,	if ye loved.
eyer sevsehler,	if they loved.

PRETERITE TENSE.

Singular.

eyer sevmishisim	if I have loved.
eyer sevmishisen,	if thou hast loved.
eyer sevmishisè,	if he has loved.

Plural.

eyer sevmishisek,	if we have loved.
eyer sevmishisiniz,	if ye have loved.
eyer sevmishisèler,	if they have loved.

PLUPERFECT TENSE.

Singular.

eyer sevsehidim,	if I had loved.
eyer sevsehiden,	if thou hadst loved.
eyer sevsehidi,	if he had loved.

Plural.

eyer sevsehiduk,	if we had loved.
eyer sevsehidiniz,	if ye had loved.
eyer sevsehidiler,	if they had loved.

FUTURE TENSE.

Singular.

eyer sevedjek olursim,	if I shall love.
eyer sevedjek olursin,	if thou shalt love.
eyer sevedjek olur,	if he shall love.

Plural.

eyer sevedjek olursuk,	if we shall love.
eyer sevedjek olursiniz,	if ye shall love.
eyer sevedjek olursaler,	if they shall love.

IMPERATIVE MOOD.

Singular.		Plural.	
sev,	love thou.	*sevelim,*	let us love.
sevsin,	let him love.	*seveniz,*	love ye.
		sevsinler,	let them love.

PARTICIPLES.

PRESENT.

Declinable.	*Indeclinable.*
seven, loving.	*sever*, loving.

PRETERITE.

Declinable.	*Indeclinable.*
sevdek, loved.	*sevmish*, loved.

FUTURE.

sevedjek, about loving.

GERUNDS.

severken, in loving.	*sevup*, having loved.
severek, while loving.	*sevendjeh*, in loving.

DEFECTIVE VERB, *im*, I am.

INDICATIVE MOOD.

PRESENT TENSE.

Singular.		*Plural.*	
im,	I am.	*iz*,	we are.
sen,	thou art.	*siz*,	ye are.
dur,	he is.	*dirler*,	they are.

PRETERITE AND IMPERFECT TENSES.

Singular.

idim,	I was, I have been.
idin,	thou wast, &c.
idi,	he was, &c.

Plural.

idek,	we were, we have been.
idiniz,	you were, &c.
idiler,	they were, &c.

&c. &c.

CONJUGATION OF THE AUXILIARY VERB
olmak, to be.

INDICATIVE MOOD.

PRESENT TENSE.

Singular.		Plural.	
im,	I am.	*iz*,	we are.
sen,	thou art.	*siz*,	ye are.
dir, der,	he is.	*dirler, derler*,	they are.

IMPERFECT TENSE.

Singular.		Plural.	
idum,	I was.	*iduk*,	we were.
iduñ,	thou wast.	*idunuz*,	ye were.
idy,	he was.	*idiler*,	they were.

PRETERITE TENSE.

Singular.

imishim,	I was or have been.
imishsiz,	thou wast or hast been.
imishdir,	he was or has been.

Plural.

imishiz,	we were or have been.
imishsiz,	ye were or have been.
imishlerdir,	they were or have been.

PLUPERFECT TENSE.

Singular.

olmish idum,	I had been.
olmish iduñ,	thou hadst been.
olmish idy,	he had been.

Plural.

olmish iduk,	we had been.
olmish idunuz,	ye had been.
olmish idiler, *olmish idy,*	they had been.

FUTURE TENSE.

Singular.

oloorim,	I shall or will be.
oloorsen,	thou shalt or wilt be.
oloor,	he shall or will be.

Plural.

olooriz,	we shall or will be.
oloorsiz,	ye shall or will be.
oloorler,	they shall or will be.

CONDITIONAL TENSE.

Singular.

oloordom,	I would be.
oloordun,	thou wouldst be.
olordy,	he would be.

Plural.

oloorduk,	we would be.
oloordunuz,	ye would be.
oloorlerdy,	they would be.

COMPOUND CONDITIONAL TENSE.

Singular.

oloormishidum,	I would have been.
oloormishiduñ,	thou wouldst have been.
oloormishidy,	he would have been.

Plural.

oloormishiduk,	we would have been.
oloormishidunuz,	ye would have been.
oloormishidiler, *oloormihleridy,* }	they would have been.

IMPERATIVE MOOD.

Singular.

ol,	be thou.
olsoon,	let him, her, or it be.

Plural.

olalem,	let us be.
olañiz or *olañ,*	be ye.
olsoonler,	let them be.

POTENTIAL MOOD.

PRESENT OR FUTURE TENSE.

Singular.

ollam,	that I may be.
ollasen,	that thou mayst be.
olla (ola),	that he may be.

Plural.

ollaooz,	that we may be.
ollasiz,	that ye may be.
ollaler,	that they may be.

PERFECT TENSE.

Singular.

olmish ollam,	that I may have been.
olmish ollasen,	that thou mayst have been.
olmish olla,	that he may have been.

Plural.

olmish ollaooz,	that we may have been.
olmish ollasiz,	that ye may have been.
olmish ollaler,	that they may have been.

IMPERFECT TENSE.

Singular.

olaidum,	that I might be.
olaidun,	that thou mightst be.
olaidy,	that he might be.

Plural.

olaiduk,	that we might be.
olaidiniz,	that ye might be.
olaleridy,	that they might be.

PLUPERFECT TENSE.

Singular.

olmish ollaidy,	that I might have been.
olmish ollaidun,	that thou mightst have been.
olmish ollaidy,	that he might have been.

Plural.

olmish ollaiduk,	that we might have been.
olmish ollaidunuz,	that ye might have been.
olmish ollaleridy,	that they might have been.

Subjunctive Mood.

PRESENT TENSE.

Singular.	*Plural.*
eyer issam, if I be.	*eyer issek,* if we be.
eyer issen, if thou be.	*eyer isseñiz,* if ye be.
eyer isseh, if he be.	*eyer isseler,* if they be.

IMPERFECT TENSE.

Singular.

eyer olsaidum,	if I were.
eyer olsaiduñ,	if thou wert.
eyer olsaidy,	if he were.

Plural.

eyer olsaiduk,	if we were.
eyer olsaiduñuz,	if ye were.
eyer olsaidiler,	if they were.

PRETERITE TENSE.

Singular.

eyer olmish issam,	if I have been.
eyer olmish issan,	if thou hast been.
eyer olmish isseh,	if he has been.

Plural.

eyer olmish issek,	if we have been.
eyer olmish issanuz,	if ye have been.
eyer olmish isseler,	if they have been

FUTURE TENSE.

Singular.

eyer olmish oloorim, if I shall be.

eyer olmish oloorsen, if thou shalt be.

eyer olmish oloor,   if he shall be.

Plural.

eyer olmish olooriz, if we shall be.

eyer olmish oloorsiz, if ye shall be.

eyer olmish oloorler, if they shall be.

INFINITIVE MOOD.

olmak, to be.

GERUNDS.

iken, being.   olidjac,   about to be.

oloop, having been. oloondjeh, whilst being.

PARTICIPLES.

PRESENT.

ollan, being.

PAST.

olmish,
imish, } having been.
oldook,

FUTURE.

oladjak,   what will be.

olmély,   what must be.

The verb " to have " is expressed in Turkish by the impersonal *var dir*, " there is," preceded by the genitive case of the possessive pronoun. Impersonal verbs have forms as follows :—

var dir, there is.	*yok dir*, there is not.
var idy, there was.	*yoghidy*, there was not.
var isseh, if there be.	*yoghissah*, if there be not.
var saidy, if there had been.	*yoghsaidy*, if there had not been.
var iken, there being.	*yoghiken*, there not being.
with other tenses from *olmak*, to be.	with other tenses from *olmamak*, not to be.

CONJUGATION OF *var dir*, to have.

INDICATIVE MOOD.

PRESENT TENSE.

Singular.

*benim var,**	I have.
senuñ var,	thou hast.
anuñ var,	he has.

Plural.

bizum var,	we have.
sizuñ var,	ye have.
anlaruñ var,	they have.

* *Id est*, " mine there is," &c.

IMPERFECT.

Singular.

benim var idy,	I had.
senuñ var idy,	thou hadst.
anuñ var idy,	he had.

Plural.

bizum var idy,	we had.
sizuñ var idy,	ye had.
anlaruñ var idy,	they had.

PRETERITE, AS THE IMPERFECT.

FUTURE.

Singular.

benim oloor,	I shall have.
senun oloor,	thou shalt have.
anun oloor,	he shall have.

Plural.

bizum oloor,	we shall have.
sizuñ oloor,	ye shall have.
anlarun oloor,	they shall have.

SECOND FUTURE.

benim oladjac,	I shall have, &c.

Conditional.

Singular.

benim oloordy,	I should have.
senuñ oloordy,	thou shouldst have.
anuñ oloordy,	he should have.

Plural.

bizum oloordy,	we should have.
sizuñ oloordy,	ye should have.
anlarun oloordy,	they should have.

Imperative.

Singular.

senuñ olsoon,	have thou.
anuñ olsoon,	let him have.

Plural.

bizum olsoon,	let us have.
sizuñ olsoon,	have ye.
anlarun olsoon,	let them have.

Optative.

present.

Singular.

benim olaidy,	that I may have.
senuñ olaidy,	that thou mayst have.
anuñ olaidy,	that he may have.

C

Plural.

bizum olaidy,	that we may have.
sizuñ olaidy,	that ye may have.
anlaruñ olaidy,	that they may have.

Preterite.

Singular.

benim olmish olaidy,	that I might have.
senuñ olmish olaidy,	that thou mightst have.
anuñ olmish olaidy,	that he might have.

Plural.

bizum olmish olaidy,	that we might have.
sizuñ olmish olaidy,	that ye might have.
anlaruñ olmish olaidy,	that they might have, &c.

So *benim yok dir,* I have not.

And *senun yok,* &c., &c.

benim yoghidi, I had not, &c.

———

These verbs are conjugated with adjectives and substantives positively, negatively, and interrogatively after the subjoined examples :—

shashmishim,	I am surprised.
zenguin dir,	he is rich.
a'alim iz,	we are learned.
meshghool idi,	he was busy.

fakir oloorim,	I should be poor.
temiz oladjaksiniz,	you will be clean.
rahat oloorler,	they should be quiet.
khabir deyil sen,	thou art not clever.
sikilmish deyil idum,	I was not troubled.
kayermaz olmaz,	he should not be heedless.
shashmish deyil misiniz,	are you not astonished ?
maghroor deyil miidy,	was he not haughty ?
sakat olmayadjakmiim,	shall I not be lame ?
laik olmazler mi idi,	should they not be worthy ?
etun var,	thou hast meat.
sharaby var,	he has wine.
suduñuz var idy,	you had milk.
kebablery oloor idy,	they would have roast meat.
bir guly yok,	he has not a rose.
aktchehmiz yok,	we have not money.
bir guemimiz yoghidi,	we have not a ship.
toozumiz olmayadjak,	we will not have salt.
yokmi bir calpaghun,	hast thou not a cap ?
yokmi idy atlarim,	had I not horses ?
mikrasim olmayadjakmi,	shall I not have scissors?

ADVERBS.

Turkish adverbs really include the adjectives, which are used adverbially ; as

khosh, nice, nicely.

eyi, good, well.

They are also made by adding *ileh*, with, or *usreh*, upon, to nouns ; as

delilik-ileh, stupidly.

dostlik-usreh, friendly.

And by adding the Arabic *an*, or the Persian *anè*, to substantives ; as

sooret-an, apparently, from *sooret*, appearance.

akibet-an, finally, from *akibet*, end.

pederanè, paternally.

Also by affixing *djeh* to express fashion or nationality ; as

Inglizdjeh, in English manner.

Farsi-dilindjeh, in the Persian tongue.

The subjoined list will be found useful as an adverbial vocabulary.

Adverbs of Quantity.

ol cadar, as much.	*pek pek*, at most.
ziadsiendjeh, too much.	*bir mikider*, a little.

vafran, abundantly.
parah parah, by pieces.
yetshir, enough.
ifrat, excessively.
ghaiet, extremely.
eksik, } less.
dakhiaz, }
azar azar, little by little.

bir az, a little.
ziadeh, } more.
artek, }
tchoc, much.
tchoc tchoc } much
dakhi ziadeh, } more.
dakha tchoc, }

Adverbs of Quality.

bed, fena, bad, badly.
dostaneh, friendly.
eyi, good.
guzel, handsomely.

nafileh, uselessly.
akel, } witty, wit-
akelaneh, } tily.
khosh, well.

Adverbs of Place.

yabandeh,   at a distance.
en dibdah,   at the bottom.
atrafdah,   around.
eiry,   across.
euyundeh,   before, in front.
ardindah,   behind, in rear.

ashaghdah,	down below.
altindeh,	down, below.
hehr yerdeh,	everywhere.
ghairy yerdeh,	elsewhere.
boondan, *shoondan,* *booradan,* *shooradjakdah,*	from, through, by this place.
andan, *oradan,* *ol yerden,*	from, through, by that place.
irak, *oozac,*	far, distant.
boondah, *shoondah,* *booradah,* *booradjak,* *shooradjakdah,*	here, in this place.
euteh beru,	here and there.
illerudeh,	in advance, in front.
guerudeh,	in the rear.
imameh,	in front.
yakin,	near,
berudeh, *boo tarafdeh,*	on this side.

orayedek,	until there.
eutedeh, } *ol tarafdeh,*	on that side.
tashradeh,	outside.
ustundeh,	on, upon.
doghroo,	straight towards.
andah, } *oradah,* *ol yerdeh,*	there, in that place.
sagdah,	to the right.
soldah,	to the left.
yokardeh,	up above.
uzreh,	upon, concerning.
itcherdeh,	within.

Adverbs of Time.

shimdilik,	at present.
tchokdan,	a long time ago.
euileyen,	at noon.
ol zemandeh,	at that time.
daima,	always.
ol sa'at,	as soon as.
ol kadar,	as long as.
sonra,	afterwards.
guidjeh,	by night.

gunduz,	by day.
evvel,	before.
akhsham,	evening.
tchin sabah,	early in the morning.
sal sal,	every year.
erken,	early.
akhsham sabah	evening and morning.
guetchinlerdeh,	formerly.
en sonra,	finally.
yawash,	gently.
shimden sonra,	henceforth.
yakindeh,	in a little time.
essky zemandeh,	in olden times.
baharin,	in spring.
yazin,	in summer.
geuzin,	in autumn.
kishin,	in winter.
apansiz,	immediately.
demin,	lately.
bildur,	last year.
guidj, kati guidjeh,	late, very lately.
shimdiden,	from this moment.
sabah,	morning (at).
shimdy,	now.
shimdiyedek,	until now.

ba'azy ba'azy,	now and then.
guidjeh gunduz,	night and day.
tchapook,	promptly.
tis tisdjeh,	quickly, quicker.
ziadeh,	sooner.
boo gun,	to-day.
yarin, *yarin ki gun,* }	to-morrow.
yarin deyil olbir gun,	the day after to-morrow.
dun deyil olbir gun,	the day before yesterday.
ertessy gun,	the next day.
euteh gun,	the other day.
sik sik,	very often.
dun, *dun ki gun,* }	yesterday.

Adverbs of Interrogation.

neh sebebden?	for what reason ?
nidjeh ?	how ?
neh kadar ?	how much ? what size ?
katche ?	how many ?
katche kerreh ? *katche def a'a ?* }	how often?
nereyeh ?	towards where ?
néréyédek ?	until where ?
katchian ?	when ?

neh ?	what ?
nitchun ?	why ?
neh shekil ? *neh vedjehileh ?* }	what kind ?
kanieh ?	where ?
neredeh ?	where ? in what place ?

Adverbs of Affirmation.

zahir,	apparently.
asslan,	absolutely.
tahkik,	certainly.
djan u guiunelden,	heart and soul.
beli, *euiler dir,* }	just so.
belki, *belkideh,* }	perhaps.
cabildir,	possibly.
olsoon,	so let it be.
guertchek,	truly, seriously.
shoobehsiz,	undoubtedly.
pek eyi, *pek guzel,* }	very well.
evet, eved,	yes.

Adverbs of Negation.

deymedeh,	I believe not.
hasha,	God forbid.

deyil,	no, it is not.
yok,	no, there is not.
neh boo var neh ol,	neither this nor that.
neh neh,	neither, nor.

Adverbs of Demonstration.

isteh,	here, behold.
bakah, *gueurkih*, }	look, look here.

Adverbs of Number.

yuz kereh,	a hundred times.
gueru, *gueneh*, }	again.
tchok kereh,	many times.
bir kereh,	once.
siktchah.	often.
tekrar,	once more.
bir dakhi,	once more.

Adverbs of Order.

neubetan, *neubetileh*, }	alternatively.
carmacarish,	any how.
evvel, *evela*, *iptida*, }	first, in the first place.

akibetan,	lastly.
bir birineh,	mutually.
sania, ⎱	second, secondly.
ikindjy, ⎰	
sira ileh,	successively.

Adverbs of Doubt.

sooretan,	apparently.
yoksah,	otherwise, if not.
belki,	probably.
olakih,	possibly.

Adverbs of Comparison.

guiby,	like, in the same way.
nidjeh,	the same as.

Adverbs of Protestation.

hai medid Allah,	God help me.
bashim itchun,	by my head.
sakilim itchun,	by my beard.

POSTPOSITIONS.

Instead of prepositions the Turks place certain words after nouns.

Those taking the nominative are—

deh, in ; thus *evdeh*, in the house.

siz, without ; thus *dostsiz*, without a friend.

uzreh, on, about ; thus *bash uzreh*, on the head.

ashrah, beyond ; thus *deniz ashrah*, beyond the sea.

Those taking the dative are —

dek, as far as ; thus *ormanehdek*, up to the wood.

carshoo, against ; thus *banah carshoo*, opposed to me.

yakin, near ; thus *evuneh yakin*, near your house.

doghroo, straight ; thus *eveh doghroo guit*, go straight home.

guereh, according to ; thus *banah guereh*, in my view.

Those taking the ablative are—

maade, besides ; thus *boondan maade*, except which.

oozac, far ; thus *dostlarendan oozac*, far from friends.

evel, before ; thus *bir aidan evel*, a month before.

euturu, concerning ; thus *boondan euturu*, about this.

sonra, after ; thus *benden sonra guel*, come after me.

bery, since; thus *iki aidan bery,* two months since.

euteh, beyond; thus *daghlerden euteh,* beyond the hills.

To these may be appended

ara,	between, among.
ard,	behind.
ashagha,	beneath.
ileri,	before.
itch,	in, amid.
itcheri,	in.
eun,	in presence.
yer,	in place, stead.
yan,	near, beside.
tashrah,	out, beyond.
taraf,	on the side.
alt,	under.
ust,	upon, on top.
yocaroo,	up, above.

CONJUNCTIONS.

The principal are as follows :—

veh,	and.
guiby,	as.

amma,	but.
amma kih,	but if.
nassilkih, zirah,	because.
zirah kih,	because that.
nitidjeh,	consequently.
illa,	except, but.
djiabah,	gratis.
neh,	however, neither.
eyer,	if.
eyer kih,	if ever.
lakin,	nevertheless.
ya, yakhod,	or, either,
andjak,	only, however.
ola kih, belki,	perhaps.
beuileh,	so.
beuileh kih,	so that.
beuileh sheuileh,	so and so.
hatta,	so much.
tchunki,	since that.
sanki,	suppose that.
euileh,	such.
kih,	that.
sheuileh iseh,	therefore.
imdi,	then.
ya 'any,	that is to say.

neh kadar kih,	whatever.
bileh,	with.
meyer,	unless.
ta,	until.
madam kih,	whilst.

EXCLAMATIONS.

The following are most in use :—

hai, eyvah,	alas !
neh yazek,	what a pity !
meded, halif,	help !
pa, okh,	oh, fine !
afferim,	well !
bakalum,	we shall see.
ai wallah,	I swear.
ba ! yok !	not at all ! no !
olmaz,	never !
savool,	take care.
alargha,	make room.
haideh,	go on (to animals).
soos,	be silent.
kess sessini,	hold your tongue.

PART II.

SYNTAX.

THE Turks address their equals or inferiors in the second person of the singular, as *khosh geldin*, thou art welcome ; but when speaking politely, they use the second person of the plural. *siz*, or some title of respect governing the third person singular, in the following manner :—

Djenabiniz or *hazretiniz dedi*, your excellency or your lordship has said.

N.B.—In complying with a wish or request, in inviting to sit, to enter, to speak, or giving and taking an order, the Turks very often use *boyou-roun*, from *bouyourmak*, to command.

The Turkish construction generally resembles the Latin.

- The nominative usually stands at the beginning of the sentence.

D

It is common to put the dative before the accusative.

The adjectives must stand before the substantives, and the genitive before the noun related to it. For instance,

eyi pashanun ogloo, the son of the good pasha.

Dependent genitives precede their substantive, and the latter adds an *i* if a consonantal, and *si* if a vowel noun ; as

o kitabin khiaghad-i,   the paper of this book.
kizin baba-si,   the father of the girl.

But if the meaning be indefinite, then the genitive sign is dropped ; as

pasha ogloo,   the son of a pasha.
dost ev-i,   the house of a friend.

But when *olmak*, to be, is used, the adjective follows the noun ; as

boo adam eyi dir,   this man is good.

When expressing number by *tchok*, much, the verb is often placed in the singular—

tchok adam geldi, a great many men have come.

Questions are asked, in absence of interrogative words, by the particle *mi ;* as

karndashin geldi mi,	has thy brother come ?
o mi, boo mi,	is it this or that ?

In replying to questions, *evet* or *beli,* yes, and
yok or *khair,* no, are used ; but it is customary to
repeat the asker's verb, thus

Q. *aghami guerdin mi,* have you seen my master ?

Ans. $\left\{ \begin{array}{l} \textit{guerdim,} \\ \textit{guermedim,} \end{array} \right.$ I have seen.
                                   I have not seen.

When one speaks about a matter of number or
weight, this must stand in the nominative, and at
the end of the phrase—

  bir partse etmek,   one piece of bread.

When the continuation of time is expressed, the
numeral must precede the object to which it
belongs, as in this example—

  besh saát okudúm, I have read five hours.

But it follows when the hour is indicated ; as

  saát besh geldi,   he came at five o'clock.

The Turkish verbs are generally followed by
the same cases of their substantives as is usual

in other languages. However, some of them require the ablative and dative; thus the verb *kork-mak*, to fear, takes *Allahdán kork*, fear God; as likewise *katchmak*, to escape; *ikrák etmek*, to hate; *koortarmak*, to deliver; *utanmak*, to be ashamed.

While *bacmak*, to see; *benzemek*, to resemble; *demek*, to say; *sormak*, to inquire; *voormak*, to strike, kill, with others, want a dative, thus

  bana bac,   look at me.

Most active and transitive verbs take a nominative as well as accusative for the object, when indeterminate; as

  sheráb itchmek,   to drink wine.

But the accusative is used, if determinate or joined to a pronominal termination, or if a proper name; as

  evimy satdim,   I have sold my house.
  Yacooby gueurdim,   I have seen Jacob.

To the question *katch, nekadar,* how much? the answer of price is given in the dative; as

  deurt grooshah,   four piastres.

As an example of Turkish construction, the Lord's Prayer is here appended :—

Gueukler deh olan Babamiz, ismiñ mooka-
Heavens in being our Father, Thy name sancti-

dess olsoon. Melekiootun guelsoon. Gueukdeh
fied let be. Thy kingdom let come. In heaven

muraduñ nidjeh iseh yerdeh dakhi beuileh. Hehr
thy will as it be in earth also so. Every

guiunkih etmekimizy bizeh boo guiun vir. Ve
daily our bread (*acc.*) to us this day give. And

sootchlarimizy baghislah bizeh sootchly-olan-
our trespasses (*acc.*) forgive towards us to the tres-

larch. Hem ighvayah salma, illa
passers (*dat.*) And to temptation (*dat.*) lead not, but

khabisden coortar. Tchun melek, koowah,
from evil (*abl.*) deliver. For kingdom, power,

isset, ebbed senun dir. Amin.
glory, eternally thine is. Amen.

PART III.

VOCABULARY OF SOME COMMON WORDS.

A.

abundance, *boluk.*
abuse, *fena aidet.*
the acacia, *sont.*
account, *hisab.*
accustom, to, *alismak.*
action, *amil.*
adder, *cara ilan.*
afternoon, *ikindy.*
agent, *vakil.*
agriculture, *tsift, djil'k.*
ague, *sitmah.*
air, *hawa.*
alone, *yaliniz.*
all, *hehr.*
almond, *badem.*
America, *Yeñ ydunia.*
an artery, *shah damar.*
anchor, *demiry.*
angels, *melekler.*
anger, *ghasib.*
antimony, *rastic.*
apoplexy, *damlah.*
apothecary, *ma'adjundju.*
apple, *elma.*
apricot, *kayissy.*
apron, *footah.*
arable land, *ishlenedjek tarla.*
architect, *mi 'mar.*

armistice, *mutarekeh.*
arms, *silah.*
the arms, *col.*
the army, *askar.*
arrival, *gidish.*
arrival, *gaelish.*
arsenal, *tersaneh.*
the ash, *dish boodak.*
ashes, *kiyeul.*
Asia, *Meshrac.*
ass, *eshek, humar.*
assault, *yurish.*
asthma, *tek nefeslu.*
attention, *ihtiraz.*
autumn, *soñ bahar.*
awake, to, *oyanmak.*
axe, *balta.*

B.

badger, *boorsook.*
baker, *ekmekdju.*
barber, *berber.*
barley, *arpa.*
barracks, *kishla.*
basin, *evornah.*
basket, *zenbil.*
baths, *hamam.*
bay, *corfez.*
bean, *bakla.*

bear, *ain*.
the beard, *sacal*.
beaver, *coondooz*.
bed, *deusek*.
bee, *ari*.
the beech, *cain*.
beef, *sighir eti*.
beer, *arpasoovi*.
beetle, *boinoozly beudjek*.
beginning, *ibtida*.
bellows, *keuruk*.
the belly, *carn*.
better, *adsi*.
bird, a, *koosh*.
birds, wild, *yeban kooshler*.
birth, *merlut*.
bit, *guiem*.
black, *siah*.
blackbird, *kara tanok*.
to blame, *zem olmak*.
blind, *keur*.
the blood, *can*.
blotting-paper, *halra kiaghidy*.
blue, *mavi*.
boar, wild, *yeban donoozy*.
the body, *roodjood*.
a bone, *guemuk*.
bootmaker, *tchizmedju*.
boots, *tchezmeh*.
bottle, *shisheh*.
boy, *oghlan*.
the brain, *beyin*.
brambles, *tsalu*.
branch, *boduk*.
brass, *toodj*.
bread, *etmek*.
break of day, *guiun aghar-masy*.
breakfast, *kafealti*.
the breast, *gugus*.
bridge, *keupry*.
bridle, *ooyan*.
bridle, *uyan*.
bronze, *pirinteh*.

broom, *supur*.
brown, *essmer*.
buckle, *coptcha*.
buffalo, *soo sighiri*.
bug, *tahtah bity*.
bull, *boogha*.
butcher, *kasab*.
butterfly, *pervaneh*.
button, *deuimeh*.
buttonhole, *ilik*.

C.

cabbage, *lahaneh*.
cable, the, *palamari*.
calf, *boozaghy*.
calf (of leg), *beldir*.
camel, *derch*.
camel-driver, *derchdju*.
cameleopard, *surnapa*.
camp, *ordoo*.
candle, *moom*.
candlestick, *shem'dan*.
cap, *fes*.
cape, *booroon*.
cap-maker, *calpaktchy*.
carpenter, *dulgher*.
carpet, *kaly*.
carrier, *hamal*.
cat, *kedy*.
caterpillar, *boe beudjeguy*.
cavalry, *atlu*.
cavern, *maghareh*.
ceiling, *tavan*.
celebrated, *namdar*.
century, a, *yuz seneh*.
certain, *gertsek*.
chair, *isskemly*.
change, to, *deyistirmek*.
charcoal, *keumur*.
chase, to, *kormak*.
cheap, *udsooz*.
cheeks, *yanaclar*.
cheese, *peinir*.
chemist, *kimiadjy*.
chicken, *pilitch*.

chimney, *odjak*.
chin, *tchcnch*.
cholic, *sandjy*.
choose, to, *sctsmek*.
cinders, *keul*.
clay, *baltchic*.
clean, *temiz*.
cloak, *yaghmoorlik*.
clock, *tchallar sa'at*.
clouds, *boolootler*.
coarse, *kalin*.
coat, *csrab*.
cobbler, *cskidjy*.
cock, *khoroz*.
coffee, *kafeh*.
coffee-house, *kafch dukiany*.
cold, *sook*.
cold, a, *zukiam*.
colour, *rung*.
colt, *tai*.
column, *dirck*.
come, to, *gelmck*.
command, to, *buyurmak*.
companion, *yoldas*.
compass, the, *poosoolah*.
compassion, *merhamet*.
complain, to, *sitiar ckmck*.
conclusion, *netidjeh*.
coufectioner, *halvadjy*.
consulate, *consoloslik*.
consumption, *rcrim*.
cook, *kebabtchy*.
cook, to, *ismak*.
copper, *bakir*.
copy, to, *tarif ekmck*.
corn-factor, *oon djy*.
cotton, *pambook*.
couch, *sofah*.
count, to, *sajmak*.
covered cart, *eurtulu araba*.
cow, *inck*.
cream, *kaimac*.
crescent, *yarcm ai*.
crocodile, *timsah*.
cross road, *arcoory yol*.

crow, *koozghoon*.
cruel, *yaruz*.
cry, to, *tshagirmak*.
cuckoo, *coocoorac*.
cucumber, *khiar*.
cunning, *akili*.
cup, *bardak*.
cup, *findjan*.
cupboard, *dolab*.
curb, *reshmch*.
curtain, *purdeh*.
cushion, *yasduk*.
custom, *adet*.
custom-house, *guiumruk*.
cut, to, *kesmak*.
cutler, *betchakchy*.
cypress, *serri aghadjy*.

D.

dates (fruit), *khoormah*.
day, *geun*.
deaf, *saghir*.
dear (in price), *pahahlu*.
dear (loved), *mahbub*.
deck, the, *anbary*.
deep, *derin*.
deer, *gueik*.
defend, to, *arka olmak*.
demand, to, *sormak*.
den, *tchih*.
departure, *guidedjek rakit*.
desert, *tchiulluk*.
desire, *arzoo*.
destiny, *tarz*.
destroy, to, *bosmak, yok et-mek*.
dig, to, *bellemek*.
disembarkation, *guemiden tchikmasy*.
dish, *tepsy*.
dismount, to, *atden inmek*.
dog, *keupck*.
door, *kapu*.
double-barrelled gun, *iky aghz'ytufcuk*.

doubt, *shoobch.*
drawers, *don.*
dress, *gucissy.*
duck, *eurdek.*
duck, wild, *yeban eurdeguy.*
dumb, *dilsiz.*
dust, *tooz.*
dwarf, *djudjeh.*
dyer, *boyadjy.*
dysentery, *itch aghrissy.*

E.

eagle, *cara coosh, kartal.*
ears the, *koolucler.*
earth, *toprak.*
earth, the, *toprac.*
east, the. *guiun doghossy.*
eat, to, *yemck.*
elder, the, *murreir aghadjy.*
elephant, *fil.*
elm, the, *cara aghadiy.*
elsewhere, *kajri yerde.*
embassy, *se'erct derlct.*
employment, *manzûb.*
end, *son.*
envelope-paper, *sarmac kiaghidy.*
envy, *iradct.*
equitable, *saha.*
evening, *aksham.*
ever so little, *azadzak.*
every, *iradct.*
everywhere, *hehryerde.*
eyebrow, the, *cash.*
eyelid, the, *kirpik.*

F.

face, *yeuz.*
fainting, *yurck bailmchsy.*
faithful, *dindar.*
falcon, *doghan.*
far, *oozak.*
farm, *bejlik.*
farrier, *na'alband.*
fat, *semiz.*

father, *baba, ata, peder.*
fear, *korkoo.*
feet, *ayaklar.*
fever, *hooma.*
field, a, *tchair.*
fig-tree, *indjir aghadjy.*
fine weather, *atchik hawa.*
finger, *parmac.*
finish, to, *bitirmck.*
the fir, *tcham.*
fire, *atesh.*
fish, *balik.*
flag, *bairac.*
flame, *'aler.*
flea, *pirch.*
flesh, *et.*
flour (wheat), *oon.*
a flower, *tchitchek.*
fly, *sinck.*
fog, *tooman.*
fold, to, *cjmck.*
follow, to, *ardina gitmek.*
folly, *deliklik.*
a ford, *guetchid.*
forehead, *aln.*
forenoon, *cushlook.*
forest, a, *orm 'n.*
forget, to, *unutmak.*
forgetfulness, *nisian.*
fork, *tchatal.*
fountain, *tcheshmeh.*
fowling-piece, *filintah, av toofenky.*
fox, *dilky.*
frog, *coorbagha.*
frost, *kiraghoo.*
fruit, *yemish.*
fruiterer, *yemishdjy.*
fruit-trees, *yemish aghadjler.*

G.

garden, *baghtche.*
gardener, *boostandjy.*
girths, *colanler.*
glass, *cadeh.*

glazier, *djamdjy.*
gloves, *eldiren.*
goat, *ketchy.*
go, to, *gitmek.*
gold, *altoon.*
goldsmith, *cooyoomdjy.*
good, *eyi.*
goose, *caz.*
gourd, *cabac.*
gout, *nikriz.*
grapes, *uzum.*
grass, *ot.*
grease, *don yaghy.*
green, *yetchil.*
gridiron, *escarah.*
grocer, *'atur.*
gun, *top.*
gunpowder, *bar ot.*

H.

hail, *tooloo.*
hair, *satch.*
half, *yari.*
half an hour, *yarem sa'at.*
halter, *yoolar.*
halting place, *dooradjac yer.*
ham, *donooz pastirmasy.*
hammer, *tchekidj.*
hand, *el.*
hare. *tavshan.*
harvest time, *orak zeman.*
hat, *calpac.*
hatchet, *baltah.*
hawk, *tchiailik.*
hay, *otlook.*
head, *bash.*
headache, *bashaghrisy.*
heart, *yurek.*
heat, *issidjac.*
heaven, *sema, geuk.*
helmit, *bashlic.*
hen, *taook.*
here is (*voici*), *ishte.*
high, *yuksek.*
highway, *oloo yol.*

hill, *bair.*
hippopotamus, *at baliguy.*
hips, *bel.*
honey, *bal.*
honour, *ikram, izzet.*
hope, *umid.*
horn, *boynouz.*
horse, *at.*
horse-dealer, *at bazukquiany*
horseshoe, *na'al.*
hospital, *bimar khanch.*
hotel, *konak.*
an hour, *bir sa'at.*
a house, *ev.*
husband, *codjia.*
hut, *kalib.*
hyena, *sertlan.*

I.

ice, *booz.*
illness, *khastalik.*
indignation, *darganlik.*
ink, *murekeb.*
in order that, *itshun.*
insect, *boudjek.*
instead of, *yerinde.*
insult, to, *azarlamak.*
in vain, *boyure.*
iron, *demir.*
ironmonger, *demirdjy.*
island, *adah.*
ivory, *fildishi.*

J.

Jesus Christ, *Hazrety 'Issah.*
jeweller, *djerahirdjy.*
join, to, *djem etmek.*
joy, *shazlik.*
jug, *bardac.*

K.

kettle, *cazan.*
key, *anaktar.*
kill, to, *culdurmek.*

kinsman, *kisim.*
kiss, to, *eupmek.*
kitchen, *matbakh.*
knee, *diz.*
knife, *bitchac.*

L.

labourer, *tchiftchy.*
lady, *kadeen.*
lake, *gueul.*
lamb, *coozy.*
lame, *topal.*
lamp, *candil.*
lantern, *faner.*
larboard, *sol yany.*
latch, *mandal.*
late, *getz.*
laundress, *tchameshirdjy.*
lead, *coorshoon.*
lean, *mide.*
leech, *senluk.*
lemonade, *elimoonatah.*
leopard, *pars.*
letter, *mektoob.*
the laurel, *defneh.*
liberty, *azadlik.*
light, *aidinlik.*
light, *noor.*
light, to strike, *ateshtchak-mac.*
lightning, *shimshek.*
the lime, *filamoor.*
linen, *bez.*
linen-draper, *asterdjy.*
lion, *arslan.*
lip, *doodac.*
little, *az, kalil.*
live, to, *yashamak.*
lock and key, *kilid anaktar.*
locksmith, *kiliddjy.*
look at, to, *bakmak.*
looking-glass, *ainah.*
love, to, *sevmek.*
low, *altshak.*

M.

maize, *misirboghdai.*
make, to, *etmek.*
man, *adam.*
mare, *kissrac.*
market-place, *tchiarshoo.*
marry, to, *evlenmek.*
matches, *kibrit.*
meat, *et.*
metal, *ma'aden.*
melon, *caroon, angur.*
merchant, *bazarguian.*
middle, *orta.*
milk, *sood.*
millet, *daroo.*
mist, *deuman.*
money-changer, *saraf.*
monkey, *meimoon.*
moon, *ai.*
morning, *sabah.*
mortar, *havan.*
mosque, *djami.*
mother, *ana.*
mount (a horse), *binmek.*
mount, to, *tsikmak.*
mountain, *dagh.*
mouse, *sitchar.*
mouth, *aghiz.*
to move, *salmak.*
much, *tchok.*
mud, *tchamoor.*
mule, *catir.*
murderer, *khirsiz.*
mushroom, *mantar.*
musket, *tufeuk.*
mustard, *khardal.*

N.

naked, *tchiblak.*
necessary, *lazim.*
needle, *inch.*
new, *yeni.*
news, *khubber.*
night, *guidjeh.*

noon, *euilch.*
nose, *booroon.*

O.

oats, *yoolaf.*
obedient, *meuteu.*
ocean, *buyuk deniz.*
odd or even, *tek tchift.*
oil, *yagh.*
olive, *zeytin.*
omelette, *kaighanah.*
order, to, *buyoormak.*
ornament, *bezek.*
ostrich, *deveh cooshy.*
otter, *soo semury.*
oven, *fooroon.*
ox, *cukuz.*

P.

pack-saddle, *semer.*
pack-saddle maker, *semerdjy.*
painter, *tasvirdjy.*
palace, *serai.*
paper, *kiaghid.*
partridge, *keklik.*
passport, *yol emry.*
pay, to, *eudemek.*
peace, *hoozoor.*
peacock, *taooz.*
pear, *emrood.*
peas, *noohood.*
pen, *calem.*
pencil, *coorshoon calem.*
pepper, *biber.*
persist, to, *dayanmak.*
pewter, *callai.*
pheasant, *suilun.*
physician, *hekim.*
pigeon, wild, *yeban gayer-djen.*
pincers, *mashah.*
pine, the, *sham.*
pistols, *tabanja.*
pitcher, *desty.*
plague, *yoomroodjac.*

plain, *kir.*
plane, the, *tchinar.*
plant, to, *dikmek.*
pleasure, *zevk.*
plunder, to, *telef olmak.*
poison, *zehir.*
poor, *fakir.*
poplar, the, *cavac.*
potato, *yer elmassy.*
powder (gun), *barook.*
pray, to, *yalvarmak.*
printer, *basmadjy.*
promise, to, *ikrar etmek.*
pulse, the, *nabs.*

Q.

quantity, *miktar.*
quarrel, *tsekish.*
question, *sooal.*
quit, to, *brakmak.*

R.

rabbit, *adu tavshan.*
radishes, *toorb.*
raft, a, *sal.*
rainbow, *yaghmoor.*
ram, *cotch.*
rat, *buyuk sitchan.*
reason, *'akil.*
receive, to, *almak.*
red, *kizil.*
reddish, *kizildjeh.*
refuse, to, *istememek.*
regret, to, *adsimak.*
reins, *dizguin.*
relate, to, *nahil etmek.*
reptile, *beudjeh.*
respect, *izzet.*
rest, to, *rahat lanmak.*
rice, *birindje.*
rich, *zenguin.*
rigging, the, *geuminuñ allaty.*
river, a, *tchai, irmak.*
roast meat, *cainamish et.*

roast, to, *kibab etmek*.
rock, *kaia*.
roof, *tam*.
room, *oda*.
rose, *gul*.
rudder, the, *dumeny*.

S.

saddle, *eier*.
saddle, to, *eierlemek*.
saddle-bags, *yandjook, hoorj*.
saddler, *seradjy*.
sailor, *kalioondjy*.
salad, *salata*.
salt, *tooz*.
sand, *coom*.
sash, *cooshak*.
save, to, *kurtarmak*.
sauce, *salsah*.
sausage, *sudjook*.
scissors, *micrass*.
sea, *deñiz*.
sealing-wax, *muhur moomy*.
seedtime, *ekin rakty*.
shark, *kenpek belighy*.
sheep, *kooioon*.
ship, *guemy*.
shirt, *guiumlek*.
shoes, *papoosh*.
shoemaker, *papooshtchy*.
shop, *dukian*.
shoulders, *oomooz*.
shovel, *atesh keruguy*.
sigh, to, *ai etmek*.
signature, *imza*.
silver, *guiumvsh*.
sink, to, *batmac*.
sister, *kiz carndash*.
skin, *dery*.
skull, *bash tchanaghy*.
sleep, *voyukoo*.
slippers, *condoorah*.
small-pox, *tchitchek*.
smell, to, *kokmak*.
smoke, *tutun*.

snail, *halezun*.
snake, *ilian*.
snow, *kar*.
son, *oghl*.
sore throat, *dolma boghaz*.
soul, *djan*.
soup, *tchorba*.
sparrow, a, *sertcheh*.
spoon, *cashic*.
spring, *bahar*.
spurs, *mahmooz*.
stable, *akhor*.
stars, the, *yuldizler*.
stern, the, *kitchy*.
stirrups, *uzenguy rikaib*.
stockings, *tchorab*.
stomach, *mi'ideh*.
stone, a, *tash*.
stove, *tara*.
stream, *irmac*.
street, *sokak*.
suddenly, *tez*.
sugar, *shaker*.
summer, *yaz*.
supper, *aksham, yemek*.
sure, *emin, gertshek*.
swan, *cooghoo*.
sword, *kilidje*.

T.

table, *sofrah*.
tablecloth, *siny bezy*.
tanner, *debbagh*.
tavern, *meikhaneh*.
tea, *tchäi*.
tears, *aghlaish*.
teeth, *dish*.
tempest, *toofan*.
tent cords, *etnab*.
tent, *tchadir*.
thread, *iplik*.
throat, *boghaz*.
thunder, *iyildirim*.
tiger, *caplan*.
time, *zeman*.

tin, *ténékch*.
trade, *zena' at*.
traveller, *yoldjy*.
tobacco, *tootoon*.
tobacco bag, *tootoon kisesy*.
tongue, *dil*.
too much, *pek tchok*.
toothache, *dish aghrisy*.
touch, to, *dokanmak*.
turn, to, *deunmek*.
turtle, *caploobagha*.
twine, *sidjim*.

U.

uniform, *birtane*.
usury, *maamale*.

V.

valiant, *ghairetli*.
valise, *djamedan*.
valley, *derch*.
vanquish, to, *getshmek*.
vapour, *bukhoor*.
veal, *tanah et*.
veil, *dulbend*.
vein, *damar*.
velvet, *kadife*.
victory, *zafer, futteh*.
vile, *altshak*.
vinegar, *sirkch*.
vintage, *bagh bozoomy*.
viper, *enguerek*.
virginity, *bikirlik*.
voyage, *yol*.
vulture, *ak-baba.*\

W.

wall, *dirar*.

want, I, *bana lazim dir*.
watch, to, *oyanik olmak*.
watchmaker, *'sa'utdjy*.
water, *soo*.
water-bottle, *tchenta*.
water-closet, *ayac yoly*.
week, a, *bir heftah*.
well, *koonoo*.
west, *baty*.
whale, *kadirgha*.
whip, *camtchy, khoorbash*.
white, *beyaz*.
wick, *fitil*.
wife, *chl*.
wind, *yel*.
window, *pendjerch*.
wine, *sharab*.
winter, *kish*.
wisdom, *hakimet*.
wish, to, *istemek*.
wolf, *koord*.
wood, *odoon*..
world, *dunia*.

Y.

yacht, *safa guemy*.
yard, the, *arli*.
year, *sen*.
yes, *evvet, beli*.
yesterday, *dun*.
yet, *daha*.
young, *guendj*.

Z.

zero, *sifr*.
zinc, *tutia ma'adeni*.

EXAMPLE OF SHORT LETTER.

Siadetloo Effendim,

Boo aksham sizeh bir ziaret etmek nyettindim. Eyer waktiniz oloorsah tezkeriyi guctirine djewab verisiniz.

ILLUSTRIOUS SIR,

This evening I have the intention to make you a visit. If you have time to receive me, be kind enough to give me an answer by bearer.

SIMPLE PHRASES.

——o——

COMPLIMENTS.

You are welcome.—*Khosh geldin.*
Good morning, sir.—*Sabah khair olsoon, effendim.*
How do you do?—*Nidjesiniz?*
How is your health?—*Keyfiniz nasil dir?*
Is your state good?—*Keyfiniz eyi mi?*
Thank God, I am well.—*Shukur Allahah, khoshim.*
Good night.—*Guedjeniz khair olah.*
The same to you.—*Khairah karshev.*
How is your father?—*Pederunuz nasil dir?*
Thank you, very well.—*Khosh booldook, pek eyi.*
He is not well.—*Eyi deil dir.*
He is dying.—*Eulur.*
He is dead.—*Euldi.*
How is your mother?—*Validehuniz nasil dir?*
She is better.—*Shifa booldi.*
May her head be preserved.—*Bashini sagh olsoon.*
I am much obliged.—*Memnounum effendim.*
May God reward you.—*Allah berekiat virsoon.*

What o'clock is it?—*Sa'at katchta?*
Nearly eight o'clock.—*Sa'at sekizch vareyar.*
Open the curtains.—*Purdurlari ásh.*

E

What trouble I give.—*Neh zahmet virirum.*

It is nothing.—*Hitch bir shay yok.*

What news is there ?—*Neh khubbar var ?*

No news.—*Khubbar yok.*

Is there good news?—*Eyi khubbar var mi ?*

The news is splendid.—*Khubbar guzel dir.*

It is bad news.—*Fena khubbar var.*

From whom did you hear it ?—*Kimden ishitdiniz mi ?*

I have not heard it.—*Ani ishitmedum.*

It is untrue.—*Yanlish dir.*

I am glad.—*Khoshnudim.*

Is it possible ?—*Mumkin mi dir ?*

It is a strange thing.—*Bir adjaib muslahat dir.*

To-day I have much business.—*Tshok ishim var boo gun.*

Give me some fresh water.—*Bir az taza soo guetir bana.*

Fill me a pipe.—*Bir chibook doldur.*

Please take it, sir.—*Bouyouroon, effendim.*

How is the weather ?—*Hawa nasil dir ?*

It is hot.—*Hawa rakid dir.*

It is cloudy.—*Boolanik dir.*

It rains.—*Yaghmoor yaghayoor.*

It is very dusty.—*Tshok toz dir.*

It is very cold.—*Pek soouk dir.*

It is dark.—*Karanlik dir.*

The moon shines.—*Mehtab var.*

It is noon.—*Euilen dir.*

Let us go to a café.—*Bir kafeych guidelim.*

Take my cloak.—*Koorkum al.*

Yes, sir.—*Evvet, effendim.*

Come here, waiter.—*Oghlan, guel boorayah.*

What do you wish ?—*Neh istersiniz ?*

Bring us coffee.—*Bizeh bir kafeh guetir.*

Will you have a cigarette ?—*Bir chigara ister-mi-siniz ?*

Have you tobacco ?—*Tutununiz var mi ?*

No.—*Khayr.*

What a pity.—*Neh yazik.*

I have some.—*Benim var.*

Bring us two pipes.—*Bizeh iki nargilleh guetir.*

Very well, sir.—*Pek eyi, effendim.*

Take this for yourself, waiter.—*Oghlan ál sana bir bakshish.*

Thanks, sir.—*Ey wallah, effendim.*

So, let us go.—*Olsoon, gidelim.*

I am going home.—*Eveh giderim.*

I must leave you.—*Sizeh terk etmely-im.*

Your servant, sir.—*Bendeniz im, effendim.*

Goodbye.—*Vidaa.*

God speed you.—*Allah yol vireh.*

God be with you.—*Allah bitendjeh olsoon.*

Is your master at home ?—*Aghan evindeh mi ?*

He is, sir.—*Evdeh, sooltanim.*

Some one wants to see you.—*Sizeh bir kimseh isteyar.*

Who is it ?—*Kim dir.*

Let him come in.—*Gelsoon itcheru.*

Rest yourself a moment.—*Bir az istirahat idersiniz.*

Holloa ! is any one here ?—*Ya! hoo bir kimseh var mi ?*

Make haste.—*Tiz eileh imdi.*

Which road must I take?—*Kanghi yoli tootmalyim ?*

How must we go to it?—*Ana yetishmeyeh nasil gitmeli iz ?*

Where does that road lead?—*Ya boo yoli nereyeh guetirir ?*

It leads to the Bosphorus.—*Karadeniz Boghazeh guetirir.*

Is it far from this?—*Boondan oozak mi?*

About four miles.—*Boondan takminen utch mil.*

I am much obliged.—*Niz pek memnoonim.*

It is very late.—*Pek guidje dir.*

How far is it to Adrianople?—*Boondan Edrenyedeh katch mil var dir?*

One hour's journey.—*Bir sa'atlik yol.*

Are there robbers?—*Khersiz var mi?*

There is no fear day or night.—*Guidje re guiunduz korku yok dir.*

Are the roads good?—*Yollar guzel mi?*

Well, friends, let us continue our journey.—*Shimdy dostlarim, yolimizeh gidelem.*

Farewell.—*Khoshdjeh kalin.*

God thank you, gentlemen.—*Allah razi olah, effendilerim.*

Summon the landlord.—*Konakdjy tchagir.*

Have you good rooms and beds?—*Eyi odalariniz re dooshekiniz var dir?*

Yes, sir.—*Evvet, effendim.*

Let us alight.—*Inélem.*

Where is the ostler?—*At-oghlan neredeh dir?*

Take our horses to the stable.—*Atlaremizeh akhorah tehekdir.*

I want refreshment, what have you?—*Ta'am etmek isterim, neh-niz var?*

What would you like, pray?—*Neh istersiniz, booyooroun?*

Have you a fowl?—*Taook-iniz var mi?*

Bring a well-cooked cutlet. — *Bir eyi pishmish kulbasti virun.*

Will you not have potatoes?—*Yerelmahsi booyoormaz misiniz?*

No, that is enough.—*Khair, ol yetishir.*

Bring me some wine.—*Bana bir az sharab guctir.*

Have you fruit ?—*Mèyve-niz var mi ?*

Bring some.—*Guctir bir az.*

This wine is good.—*Boo sharab eyi.*

The meat is not well dressed.—*Et eyi pish-me-mish.*

Where are our servants ? — *Khitmutkiarler-imiz khandeh devler ?*

Supper (table) is ready.—*Sofra kooroolmish dir.*

Bed is better than supper.—*Dooshek bana sofraden eyi dir.*

Light the gentlemen.—*Effendilereh moom tutun.*

Good night.—*Guidjeniz khayr olah.*

What is to pay ?—*Boordjoomiz neh kadar dir ?*

Give what pleases you.—*Istediyinizi verin.*

Give me twenty-five piastres.—*Yirmi besh ghoroush verin.*

Waiter, here are twenty paras.—*Ya oghlan, ál sana yirmi para.*

May God repay you.—*Allah inayet eileyeh.*

Do not answer me.—*Djewab yok.*

I am angry.—*Durilmish im.*

It is nothing.—*Hitch bir shay yok.*

Hold your tongue.—*Soosiniz.*

I am not pleased with you.—*Sizden khooshhnud deil-im.*

Is there any hot water ?—*Kainar soo var mi ?*

Give me some soap.—*Bir az saboon vir.*

Light the fire.—*Ateshi yak.*

Pour out cold water.—*Soouk soo deuk.*

Are my boots clean ?—*Tchismelerimi temiz ?*

What coat will you have to-day?—*Kanghi esbabi guiersiniz boo guiun ?*

Give me my cap.—*Kalpaghimi ver.*
Let us go out.—*Tchikalim.*
Breakfast is ready.—*Kahfeh alti hazir.*
Does the water boil?—*Soo kainar mi?*
Bring two cups and saucers.—*Bana iki tass ileh zarf guetir.*
Take more cream.—*Daha kaimak ál.*
Bring new-laid eggs.—*Taza yoomoortah guetir.*
What have we for dinner to-day?—*Boo guiun yemek-deh neh-miz var?*
Have we any fish?—*Balighimiz var mi?*
There is game.—*Shikiar rar.*
At what hour do you wish to dine?—*Sa'at katehdeh yemekdeh istermisiniz?*
Dinner is ready.—*Sofra koroolmish dir.*
I will take some roast meat.—*Kebabden bir az alirim.*
It is delicious.—*Pek lezetloo dir.*
I drink to your health.—*'Ashkinizch itchiurem.*
Best wishes.—*'Afietler otsoon.*

Where are you going?—*Neredych gideyorsiniz?*
Is there a boat?—*Kaik boldoon mi?*
Here it comes.—*Ishte! gueliur.*
Is all ready?—*Hehr shay hazir mi?*
All ready, sir.—*Hazir dir, effendim.*
Please get into the boat.—*Kaikah guirin booyooroon.*
Give way, my lads.—*Hai kardashlarim, tshek doghroo.*
Shall we go on shore?—*Inelim mi?*
Have we any more wine?—*Dakhi sharabimiz var mi?*
I hope it will not rain.—*Allah vireh yaghmayaidi.*
I do not think it will rain.—*Deimedeh ki yagha.*
I have no powder.—*Barootim yok dir.*
Here it is.—*Ishte dir.*
Have you bullets?—*Koorshunin var mi?*

Is there any game in this country?—*Boo etrafdeh av var mi?*

This wood is full of game.—*Boo orman av top toloo dir.*

Fire.—*Atiniz.*

I have hit it.—*Ben oordoom.*

Give the servants the game to carry.—*Toofeukleri khismetkiarlarah virunuz guetirsunler.*

Let us enter this shop.—*Shoo dukianch quirelim.*

What do you look for?—*Neh ararsiniz?*

I want some fine cloth.—*Bir guzel tchioka istérim.*

Here is excellent cloth.—*Ishte bir eyi tchioka.*

I want a dark colour.—*Kooyoo rengi istérim.*

How do you sell it?—*Katchia virirsiniz?*

Three piastres a yard.—*Utch groushah arshooni.*

Is it true what is said of the Pasha?—*Pashaden uturu didikleri guertchek mi dir?*

What is said!—*Neh dirler?*

That he is disgraced.—*M' azool olmish didiler.*

His fall will be cause of much trouble to many.—*Anun m'azool oldooghy tshok adamah zarar gueturur.*

You are quite right.—*Guertchek sen.*

Well! let us go.—*Ey, gidelim.*

PRINTED BY BALLANTYNE, HANSON AND CO.
EDINBURGH AND LONDON.